ROCK ON BILLY

by Jake Handler

Illustrations John McNees

PAGE PUBLISHING, INC.
New York, NY

First originally published by Page Publishing, Inc. 2017

Illustration, Cover Design and Layout by John McNees (nowillustrationanddesign.com)© 2017

ISBN 978-1-64027-860-8 (Paperback)
ISBN 978-1-64027-861-5 (Digital)

Printed in the United States of America

To my parents

For providing me with the
education, resources, and love
throughout my life
to make this opportunity possible

Billy is an adventurous boy,
On his eighth birthday he received a toy.

It wasn't a video game or even a car.
In fact, it was an acoustic guitar.

At first Billy really struggled,
All the notes and chords were juggled.
But Billy worked harder and
pursued his dream,
To shine as a star in his own gleam.

Billy worked out the kinks
all day and all of the night,
His rock star future was looking bright.

So one day Billy was headed for the doors,
The music world he was about to explore.
He decided to trek on a journey for fame,
All he had was his guitar to his name.

Billy walked through his
small town once or twice,
Searching for some career advice,
Until finally he saw critters
that looked like lice!

"Our names are John, Paul,
George, and Ringo,
We like to dance and we like to sing-o!
Even though we're just
insects on the ground,
Our music is internationally renowned.
We are the beetles and we are from Britain,
What type of music have you written?"

"I write all types of music!" said Billy.
"Some soft, some loud,
some sad, some silly!
One day I hope to be a famous rock star,
So I can soar with the birds
And fly away real far!"

"Well, mate, you are in the wrong place,
you are looking for the ones with a
beak on their face."

"They really like bread, but
they are not seagulls.
They fly over hotels; they are the eagles."

So the beetles gave Billy some direction,
On how to pursue his road to perfection.
Billy traveled through Abbey Road
and down Penny Lane,
But suddenly it began to rain.
"Darn!" yelled Billy. "No eagles will fly,
Birds don't like the rain;
they like to be dry!"

16

Although the eagles were already gone,
Billy was motivated to dream on.
So he walked along the sticks and stones,
Arriving at a wilderness unknown.
Alone in the woods, Billy began to shake.
He saw turtles, scorpions, and even
a white snake.

There was a dust in the wind,
And the weather was wavy.
Billy gazed ahead and saw his friend Davy.
"Davy! Davy!" Billy screamed.
"I am lost along the river of dreams!"

"Billy! Come here and meet my friends!
They are Michael, Peter,
and Micky Dolenz."

"Hey, hey, we're the monkeys,
on the trees we swing.
Sometimes we act, sometimes we sing!"

"Can you make me famous?" Billy replied.
"Ugh!" The monkeys sighed.
"We tried and we cried, we
looked far and wide,
but that idea has gratefully died."

"You must work hard to be an achiever.
You can do it, Billy. I'm a believer!"
"Before you think your hopes
are destroyed,
You should speak to my pal;
his name is Floyd."

Billy thought that was great news,
Meeting Floyd – he couldn't refuse.

The rain stopped and there was
a bad moon rising.
Billy looked ahead into the horizon.

Floyd was dressed in all pink,
Not recognizing Billy, he had to blink.
"Who are you?" Floyd shouted,
With a vision that was clouded,
"Hey you!"
Billy pouted.

"I want to be famous and
I love rock 'n' roll,
Can you help me achieve my goal?"
Billy asked with a petty soul.
"I spoke to the animals, but
finally I'm seeing,
Someone like me…a human being!"

"I will lead you toward the right direction,
But you know, you can't rush perfection.
You should speak with Bruce, he's the boss,
Do you see the river? He lives right across."

"Listen to me and follow my plan,
I am a very wise old man.
I'm sure he could help you on your quest."
"Yes!" shouted Billy. "You are the best!"

So Billy walked through the badlands
and down Thunder Road,
He had traveled so far,
he was in another zip code.
It appeared Billy had been lost,
He wanted help but at what cost?

Suddenly Billy began to think,
About the beetles, the monkeys,
and Floyd dressed in pink.
They didn't get famous by asking others,
Friends, siblings, fathers, mothers.
They worked hard in order to succeed,
That self-motivation is what I need!

Behind blue eyes,
Billy realized…
Only I can control my own fate,
Every night I will practice till late,
And I will make *myself* great.
But for now…I'm only eight!

Billy's new friends he would surely miss,
But it was time to go give his mom a kiss.
As he was walking home,
it was getting chilly,
One day the crowd will roar and scream…

About the Author

Inspired by a short story created while in the fourth grade, author and classic music lover Jake Handler wrote *Rock on Billy* at the age of 22. In addition to writing children's books, the New Jersey-born author is a physical education teacher, coach, and community volunteer. Jake currently resides in Baltimore, Maryland, where his creative mind is striving to create a series of sequels to *Rock on Billy*. For more information about the book and its author, follow @rockonbilly on Twitter.

CPSIA information can be obtained
at www.ICGtesting.com
Printed in the USA
LVOW05s0408210218
567365LV00009B/15/P